ALPHATORTS
WITH X-TRA YUMMY ZUCCHINIS

By Hugh Willard

Illustrations by Lynda Farrington Wilson

ALPHATORTS
WITH X-TRA YUMMY ZUCCHINIS

Contact Hugh Willard at www.alphatorts.com

Illustrated by Lynda Farrington Wilson
www.lyndafarringtonwilson.com

ISBN 978-0-615-35124-7

FOREWARD

A note to the adult kids

Alphatorts are first and foremost created to be fun and whimsical. Beyond the whimsy however, alphatorts are designed to facilitate critical thinking in the arena of language, and vocabulary expansion. I see this as being supremely relevant and needed in our age of warp speed communication technology, wherein we take more and more shortcuts (omg; lol) and use monochromatic vocabulary. We are losing the refined art of language within communication.

So, what exactly is an alphatort? Well, it is a sentence, or two or three, that uses each letter of the alphabet, in order, with grammatical and contextual coherence. O.k., I take a little license with the contextual coherence (a little, not excessively so, for this often provides the fun). It forces the writer to work for meaning in an often light and fun way. It becomes enzymatic for the reader in the process of expanding critical language and vocabulary development. The alphatorts within this compilation are for kids of all ages, allowing for a minimal foundation of language construction and vocabulary development likely to be found among most students by the third grade. Alphatorts can be calibrated for older persons as well (e.g. "Although Barely Christened Daylight, Each Fair Gladiola Harkens Incantations, Joyous Kaleidoscopic Laudations, Memorable Now Of Picturesque Quixotic Redolent Sacral Transmutations, Ubiquitously Venerating Wayward Xanadu Yearnings Zestfully."), and can range from the silly, to the poetic, and the sublime.

I hope you and your young children and friends enjoy these alphatorts as much as I did in creating them. I would like to add my special gratitude here for Lynda Farrington Wilson. Her illustrations breathed a magical life into the words and characters in this book. Maybe you can try your own hand, and mind, at making your own.

Happy reading,

Hugh J. Willard

All Baseball Coaches Dearly Enjoy Fireball
Game Heroes In July, Keeping Loud-Mouth
Nosey Opposing Pitchers Quiet Remembering
Smashes Till Umpires Vamoose With
X-tra Yummy Zucchinis.

Are Bumbling Clowns Doing
Elastic Flying Gymnastic
Hops Inside Jalopy Kars
Lacking Mental Nuggets?

Or Possibly Quick Reasonably
Serious Theatre Understudies
Visiting With X-tra Yummy Zucchinis.

3

Ally Beat Chelsea Doing Easy Frog Game
Hopping In Jumpy Kicking Leaps Masking New
Original Pounces, Quirkily Repairing Sneaker
Tops Using Vines With X-tra Yummy Zucchinis.

4

Although Big Children Dine Elegantly,
Fairy Godmothers Hurry Inside Jumbo Kitchens,
Laughing, Muttering Nonsense Over Preparing
Quality Ravioli So Tots Upstairs
Visit With X-tra Yummy Zucchinis.

Awaken Bored Children! Don't Ever Feel
Glum Having Inside Jobs Keeping Long
Magnificent November Office Plants Quenched.
Recollect Silly Tales Until Vamoosing
With X-tra Yummy Zucchinis.

A Big Cat Driver Each Friday Goes Hunting In
Jungle Khakis, Lugging Monkeys Needing Oily

Papayas **Q**uietly **R**iding **S**pare **T**ires **U**nder
Vehicles **W**ith **X**-tra **Y**ummy **Z**ucchinis.

Aliens Burping Comets, Divide Earth, Flinging
Gassy Heat Inside Jupiter, Kindly Leaving
Mercury, Neptune, Orion, Pluto Quietly
Revolving Saturn, Trolling Uranus,
Venus With X-traterrestrial Yummy Zucchinis.

Ali Baba Calls Desert Edible Flowers Gross,
Harboring Insects Jumping, Knowing Long
Moroccan Nights Overwhelm Pachyderms
Quickly Revealing Stubby Tootsies Under Velvet
With X-tra Yummy Zucchinis.

Anyone But Crying Donkeys Eating Fruit
Gummies Hates Iced Jellybeans Melting Near
Old Pig Quarters, Really Smelling Terrible,
Unleashing Vapors With X-tra Yummy Zucchinis.

And Before Calling Ducks Equal, First Gather
Hundreds In Jubilation, Kneeling, Listening
More Nervously Over Potential Quacks
Resetting Sound Toots Underwater Verses
Winging X-tra Yummy Zucchinis.

Along Briar Creek, Dogs Eagerly Frolic,
Going Hounding In Jittery Kicks Like Maniacs

Nervously Panting Quite Rumbly Stumbly Tumbly
Uncovering Voles
With X-tra Yummy Zucchinis.

Are Bugs Crunchy?
Do Elephants Fall Gently?
How Is Jell-O Knotted?
Large Mosquitoes Niggle Oinking Pigs?
Quite Right Says Those Uptight Voters With
X-tra Yummy Zucchinis.

Alligators Believe Crocodiles Devour Entire Fish
Grits Hot. Instead June Kiwi Leaf Munchies,
Not Overcooked, Pleasantly Quiet
Reptiles Sour Tummies, Upchucking
Vittles With X-tra Yummy Zucchinis.

11

About Bedtime, Children Denying Entrance

For Grizzlies Hibernating Inside January Kleenex

Leave Mostly New Opossums

Pawing Quiverishly Retracing Steps Toward Unusual Varmints Wanting X-tra Yummy Zucchinis.

Amazing Beyond Compare, Derrick Entered
Fourth Grade Having Ingested Jellybean
Kibbles, Licking, Munching New Onion
Pimento Quiches Regularly, Slowly
Turning Uniquely Violet Without
X-tra Yummy Zucchinis.

Along Blueberry Court, Doughnuts Enlarge
Fancy Giant Hammocks Inside Jelly Kreme
Licorice Making Noggins Overly Plump
Quickly Reversing Slimming
Techniques Until Visits

With X-tra
Yummy Zucchinis.

Anyone Believing Christmas Day Eight
Flying Gift Hoofers Inspect
Just Kids Letters, Must Not
Open Presents Quickly,
Recalling Santa Treats
Unusual Visitors
With X-tra
Yummy
Zucchinis.

Dear Santa, I am a good boy

TO SANTA NORTH POLE

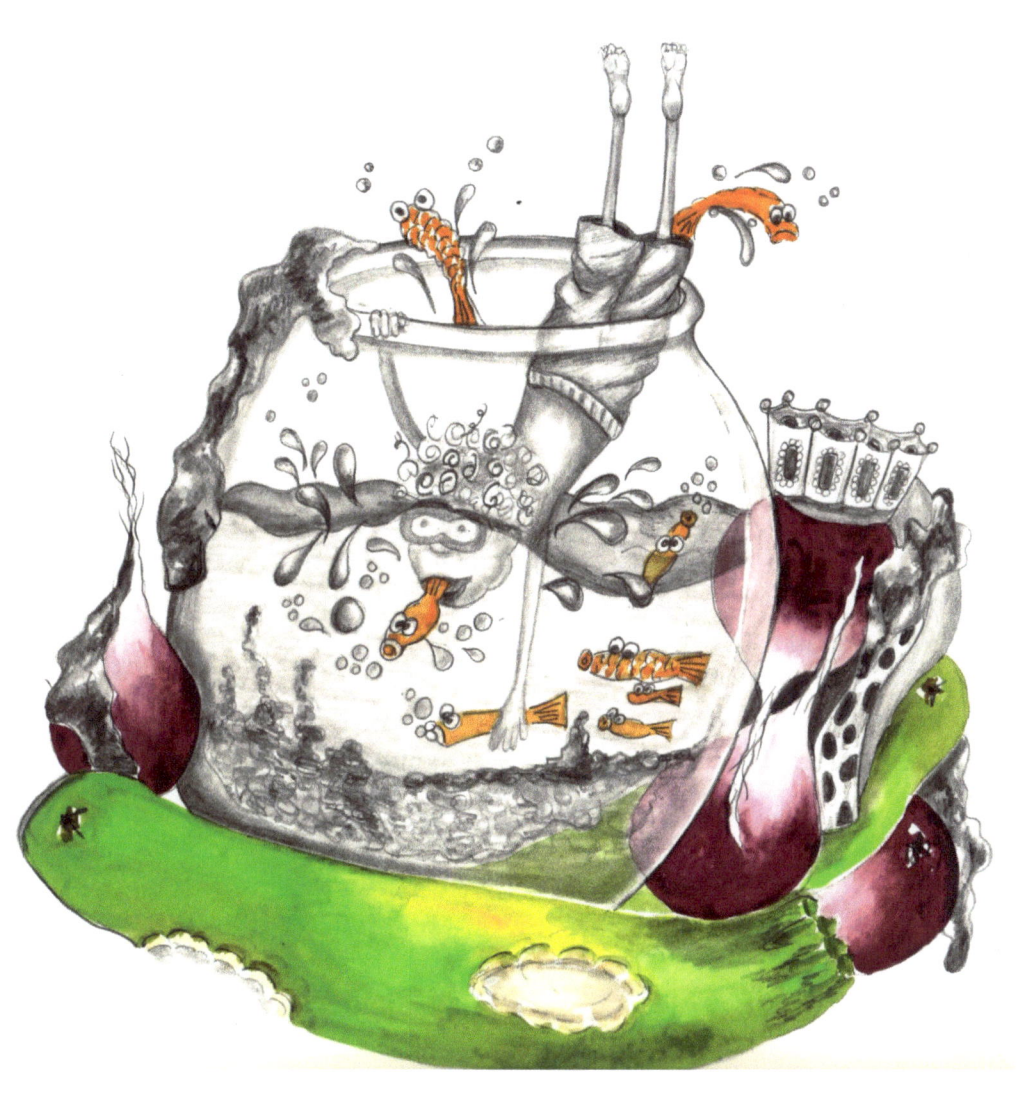

Any Bright Child Doesn't Eat Fried Guppies.

However Impossibly Juicy Kelp Looks

Much Nicer On Purple Queens Radishes,

So Try Uncooked Vegetables

With X-tra Yummy Zucchinis.

www.ingramcontent.com/pod-product-compliance
Lightning Source LLC
Chambersburg PA
CBHW040902120626
46551CB00001B/125